D1487740

MONSTER AND Frog

And the

TERRIBLE TOOTHACHE

For Rosa
R.I.

For my dad (Florida 2005)
R.A.

Consultant: Prue Goodwin,
Lecturer in literacy and children's books,
University of Reading

ORCHARD BOOKS
338 Euston Road, London NW1 3BH
Orchard Books Australia
Hachette Children's Books
Level 17/207 Kent Street, Sydney NSW 2000

First published in Great Britain in 2006
First paperback publication 2007

Text © Rose Impey 2006
Illustrations © Russell Ayto 2006

The rights of Rose Impey to be identified as the author and
Russell Ayto to be identified as the illustrator of this Work
have been asserted by them in accordance with the
Copyright, Designs and Patents Act, 1988.

A CIP catalogue record for this book is available from the British Library

ISBN 1 84121 534 1 (hardback)
ISBN 1 84362 227 0 (paperback)

1 3 5 7 9 10 8 6 4 2

Printed in China

MONSTER AND frog

And The

TERRIBLE TOOTHACHE

ROSE IMPEY  RUSSELL AYTO

ORCHARD BOOKS

Monster has a terrible toothache.

But he will not go to the dentist.
Monster thinks it might hurt.

Monster does not know what
to do.

But Frog knows. He is full of ideas.
"We must pull that tooth out,"
he says.

Monster does not like that idea.

"You will not feel a thing," says Frog. "Trust me. I know all about pulling out teeth."

First, Frog ties a piece of string
round Monster's tooth.
Then he pulls hard on the string . . .

and harder . . .

and harder.

Suddenly, Frog flies across the
room like a yo-yo.
He hits Monster in the eye.
"Ow!" yells Monster.

That hurt!

Poor Monster. Now he has
a toothache *and* a black eye.
"Do not worry," says Frog.
"I have another idea."

This time, Frog ties the end of
the string to the door handle.

He closes the door with a BANG!

CRAAASH! The door falls on Monster's head.

"Owwwww!" yells Monster.

Now Monster has a toothache, a black eye, *and* a bump on his head.

But Frog knows how to cheer
him up.
"We will go for a walk," he says.
"Walking always gives me ideas."

Outside the house they see
Monster's car.

Frog ties the string to the bumper.
"I hope this will not hurt,"
says Monster.

"Do not worry," says Frog, as he drives away.

"This is one of my better ideas."

Brrrmmmmmmmm!

But Monster's tooth is so strong
it pulls the bumper off the car.

It lands on Monster's foot.

"Ow! Ow! Ow!" cries Monster,
hopping around.

Now Monster has a toothache,
a black eye, a bump on his head
and a squashed foot.

"Cheer up, Monster," says Frog.
"We will soon have that tooth out."
Down the road they pass
a building site.

Outside is a big red steamroller.

"Now *that* is just what we need,"
says Frog.
"Are you sure?" says Monster.

"Trust me," says Frog. "This is
my best idea yet."

Frog ties the string to the steamroller.
He jumps into the driver's seat and
starts the engine.
But, oh, no!

The steamroller is in reverse!
It runs backwards, over Monster's
tail and rolls it flat, like a piece
of pastry.

o-www!

Poor Monster sits down at the side of the road and bursts into tears.

"Do not cry, old friend," says Frog. "I have lots more ideas yet."

"Please," says Monster, "no more ideas. I would rather have toothache!"

Just then along comes
Monster's sister.
"Hello, Monster! Hello, Frog!"
she says. "Whatever is wrong?"

Monster tells her that he has
a flattened tail,

a squashed foot,

a bump on
his head,

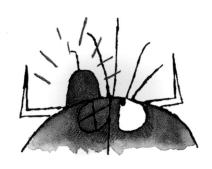

a black eye,

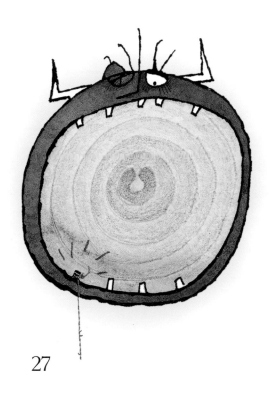

and a
terrible
toothache.

"At least we can get rid of the
toothache," says Monster's sister.
"We can go to the dentist."
Monster still does not like that idea.

"Dentists do not hurt," says his sister.

"Don't they?" says Monster.

"Of course not," says Frog.

"Everybody knows *that!*"

The dentist makes sure that Monster's mouth is numb.

Then he pulls out the tooth. Soon Monster's toothache has gone.

"Going to the dentist *was* a good idea," says Monster. "Yes," says Frog. "It is a good job I thought of it. I am full of good ideas."

MONSTER AND Frog

ROSE IMPEY 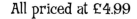 RUSSELL AYTO

Enjoy all these adventures with Monster and Frog!

All priced at £4.99

Orchard Colour Crunchies are available from all good bookshops, or can be ordered direct from the publisher: Orchard Books, PO BOX 29, Douglas IM99 1BQ
Credit card orders please telephone 01624 836000
or fax 01624 837033 or visit our Internet site: www.wattspub.co.uk
or e-mail: bookshop@enterprise.net for details.

To order please quote title, author and ISBN
and your full name and address.
Cheques and postal orders should be made payable to 'Bookpost plc.'
Postage and packing is FREE within the UK
(overseas customers should add £1.00 per book).

Prices and availability are subject to change.

ORCH
OL
CRUN

Monster and Frog are the best of friends.
Monster does not know very much, but Frog
thinks *he is an expert on everything...*

Monster is scared to go to the dentist,
even though he has a terrible toothache.
Frog says he will help, he is an
expert at pulling out teeth...

£4.99

ISBN 1-84362-227-0

9 781843 622277